A NORTH-SOUTH PAPERBACK

Critical praise for

Mary and the Mystery Dog

"This book tells a simple, satisfying tale with immediacy and humor. Children will enjoy the pleasing animal story, illustrated with watercolor paintings that conjure up the feelings of the characters and the feel of a wet cold day by the ocean. A rewarding short choice for children just a bit beyond the beginning readers stage." *Booklist*

"Sketchy watercolors on every spread suit the breezy, light text. Subject, format, and art work together to make this a fine story for emerging readers." *The Horn Book Guide*

Mary

and the

Mystery Dog

By **Wolfram Hänel**

Illustrated by

Kirsten Höcker

Translated by J. Alison James

North-South Books

New York · London

First published in the United States, Great Britain, Canada,
Australia, and New Zealand in 1999 by North-South Books,
an imprint of Nord-Süd Verlag AG, Gossau Zürich, Switzerland.
First paperback edition published in 2000 by North-South Books.

Distributed in the United States by North-South Books Inc., New York.

Library of Congress Cataloging-in-Publication Data
Hänel, Wolfram
[Willi der Strandhund. English]
Mary and the mystery dog / by Wolfram Hänel ; illustrated by
Kirsten Höcker ; translated by J. Alison James.
Summary: Mary and her parents meet a friendly dog
when they go to the beach for a week.
[1. Dogs—Fiction. 2. Beaches—Fiction.] I. Höcker, Kirsten,
ill. II. James, J. Alison. III. Title.
PZ7.H1928Mar   1999
[E]—dc21   98-42104

A CIP catalogue record for this book is available from The British Library.

ISBN 0-7358-1043-5 (trade binding)
1 3 5 7 9 TB 10 8 6 4 2
ISBN 0-7358-1044-3 (library binding)
1 3 5 7 9 LB 10 8 6 4 2
ISBN 0-7358-1337-X (paperback)
1 3 5 7 9 PB 10 8 6 4 2
Printed in Belgium

For more information about our books,
and the authors and artists who create them,
visit our web site: www.northsouth.com

Mary and her parents were going to spend a week at the beach.

It was still March and rather cold, but Mary's mother said, "It doesn't matter how bad the weather is if you are prepared."

So she packed a thick pullover for each of them, and their raincoats and boots, and off they went to their house by the sea.

When they got there, Mary's father settled himself in front of the fireplace, and Mary's mother curled up on the sofa to read a book. Mary wanted to explore.

"Can we go to the beach and see what the waves brought in during the night?" she asked.

"Too cold," said Father.

"Too windy," said Mother.

"Then I'll go alone," said Mary, and she pulled on her rubber boots.

Outside it really *was* cold. Heavy dark clouds chased one another across the sky. The wind whistled and whipped at Mary's raincoat. She struggled up the dunes . . . and then there it was—the whole ocean right in front of her!

The sea spray shone white and the surf thundered like a train. Not a soul was on the beach. Only Mary.

Mary walked up close to the water's edge. There the sand was heavy and damp and the stones glistened.

There were treasures everywhere: crab claws and lots of shells—mussel and oyster shells and even a whole conch.

Mary saw an empty bottle. She thought it might have a message inside. She spotted a feather; it was probably from an eagle.

A row of gulls squatted at the water's edge. They were waiting to see what the waves would wash up at their feet.

Mary ran straight at the gulls, waving her arms and shouting, "I'm going to get you! I'm going to get you!"

Screeching, the gulls flapped into the air and were carried off by the gusty wind.

All at once the sun came out from behind the clouds. Mary pulled off her boots and her thick socks. But the sand was still much too cold to go barefoot! Mary hopped on one leg and tried to get her boots back on again without sitting down.

Suddenly Mary saw something move over
in front of the dunes. She held her breath
with excitement.

It was some kind of animal.

A large, furry animal.

At least as large as a bear.

And now the animal was bounding right
at her!

Mary quickly looked the other way. She acted as if she were just walking along, as if she were only on the beach by chance. She pretended she'd never seen the animal.

But then it was at her side, and barking! It was a dog. And he seemed quite friendly, even though he was so big.

"For goodness' sake!" cried Mary. "I know who you are. Look at you!" Mary had read stories about the Mystery Dog who lived all alone at the beach, in a hut behind the dunes. He was very shaggy, just like this dog here.

"Hello, boy," said Mary.

The dog barked twice and wagged his tail.

"It's really you," cried Mary. "Want to play?"

The dog tilted his head and wagged his tail again.

Mary ran down the beach with the dog barking at her heels. She found a stick and threw it high in the air. The dog caught it and brought it back.

Then Mary threw the stick out into the waves. The dog plunged into the water and brought the stick back. Mary ran in circles. The dog did too. Mary did a handstand, a cartwheel, and flopped in the sand and rolled over and over.

The dog rolled onto his back and kicked all four paws in the air.

Finally the two of them sat down in the sand
completely out of breath. The dog tilted his
head to the side and wagged his tail.

"We'll play again in a second," said Mary, and she rubbed his thick fur, which was full of sand and saltwater. "I just need to catch my breath."

Then they saw Mary's father coming. They could see him far in the distance, leaping to avoid the waves, his raincoat flapping in the wind.

He looks like a gull, thought Mary. Like a
huge gull just learning to fly. Mary giggled.

The dog pricked up his ears.

"Don't worry," said Mary. "It's only my
father." But the dog had already bounded off
into the dunes.

"What was that?" asked Mary's father when he finally reached her.

"That was the Mystery Dog!" cried Mary excitedly. "You know, the dog from all those stories! He really exists!"

"Nonsense," said Father. "Besides, I don't want you playing with strange dogs."

"But he isn't a strange dog," Mary tried to explain. "He's the Mystery Dog."

"Humph," grumbled Father. "Come on now, it's time to go home. Mother has lunch ready."

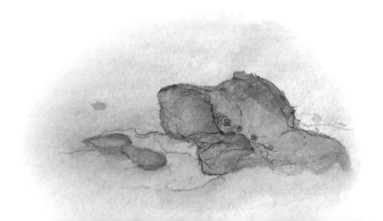

Mary followed behind her father as they trudged through the sand. The wind pushed and pulled, as if it wanted to blow them right across the beach. Mary looked around, but the dog was nowhere to be seen.

For lunch there were sausages and mashed potatoes. But Mary wasn't very hungry. The whole time she was thinking about the dog. "It really is him," she said. "Believe me. He looks exactly the same, and he lives all alone on the beach in a hut somewhere out in the dunes."

Mary's mother said, "I suppose this means we all need to take a look at your dog."

"Come on then!" said Mary, jumping up.

"This is where we were!" called Mary when they reached a pail half full of sand.

"So where is the dog?" Mother asked.

"I don't know," said Mary. "You wait here while I look for him."

"I hope it doesn't take too long," said Mother, shivering from the cold.

"I hope the fire back home doesn't go out," grumbled Mary's father impatiently.

I hope I can find him, thought Mary as she trudged through the dunes.

Then suddenly there he was, standing in front of her. He tilted his head to the side and wagged his tail, just as if he'd been waiting for her.

"Come with me," said Mary. "I have to show you to my parents. They don't believe you're real."

She ran down the high dunes and took off running with the dog close behind.

"Here he is!" Mary called to her parents. "See, just like I told you!"

The dog bounded towards Mary's parents. Then he stopped short, barked a couple of times, and suddenly plunged into a puddle of water.

Mother was able to jump aside.

But Father wasn't quick enough; he was sprayed from head to toe.

The dog was all set to splash in the puddle again when Mary's father yelled, "Sit!"

And the dog sat down.

"Lie down!" ordered Father. The dog lay down in the sand. "I know how to handle dogs," said Father proudly.

"Now stand up again," he said. "Up, now!"

The dog jumped up high. Before Father knew what was coming, he had a wet paw on each shoulder.

And a rough dog tongue licking his face.

Mary's father was so surprised, he lost his balance. He flapped his arms wildly and then fell right in the puddle!

"You certainly know how to handle dogs," said Mary's mother, laughing.

Yapping, the dog bounced around Father,
almost knocking him flat.

Suddenly a scooter came roaring over the beach. The man on it was calling something.

They couldn't understand a word until the man had turned off the engine and there was only the sound of the birds and the wind.

"Can I help you?" said Father, standing
up and brushing the sand off his jeans.

"I just wanted to get my dog," said the
man.

40

"He's *your* dog?" asked Mary.

"Yes," said the man. "I always leave him here in the mornings when I go out on the boat to fish, because he gets seasick. I pick him up in the afternoon."

"But doesn't he live here at the beach?" asked Mary. "In a hut on the dunes?"

"No," the man said with a laugh. "We live in the next village, a little way down the beach. And now we have to get home. I have a couple of good cod fish here that I want to cook for supper. Up, boy. Hop up!"

The dog jumped onto the seat, and they headed off.

Mary looked sadly at her parents. "He wasn't the Mystery Dog after all," she said. But then the dog barked a good-bye and Mary laughed.

"But at least our week at the beach is sure to be fun," said Mary. "I can play with the dog every day. And the two of you can stay in the house and keep warm."

"No way," said Father. "I'm coming too. It's my turn to wrestle him to the ground. Just you wait and see."

"I don't believe it," said Mother.

"You'll have to come too, then," declared Mary. "To see for yourself."

All three of them burst out laughing. And then Mary pushed her father down in the sand, just like the Mystery Dog had done!

About the Author

Wolfram Hänel has lived for most of his life in Hannover, Germany. He studied German and English literature and has worked as a photographer, a graphic artist, a copywriter, a teacher, and a playwright. Wolfram Hänel, his wife, and their daughter live in Hannover and Kilnarovanagh, Ireland. The story about the Mystery Dog actually happened to them on a trip to the North Sea.

About the Illustrator

Kirsten Höcker was born in a small town near Osnabrück, Germany. She studied art history and later went into illustration at the Berlin School of Fine Arts. Since graduating, she has created illustrations for picture books, children's television shows, and newspapers and magazines. Kirsten Höcker lives in Berlin and in Metz, France. Since she grew up on a farm, the stories she likes best are about animals.

Other North-South Easy-to-Read Books